# Matthew Gollub

# UNCLE SNAKE

PICTURES BY

## Leovigildo Martínez

**TORTUGA PRESS**

Santa Rosa, California

Printed in China by South China Printing Company Ltd.
The text type is Carmina. The illustrations were painted in watercolor on textured paper.
Glaze was used to achieve the distinctive shades of color.

Library of Congress Cataloging-in-Publication Data
Gollub, Matthew. Uncle Snake/ by Matthew Gollub; pictures by Leovigildo Martínez. p.  cm.
Summary: When his face is changed into that of a snake after he visits a forbidden cave, a young boy wears a mask
for twenty years, before being taken into the sky.
[1. Folklore—Mexico. 2. Lightning—Folklore.] I. Martínez, Leovigildo, ill. II. Title
PZ8.1.G6356Un 2004 [398.2'0972'06]—dc20 LCCN 2004094729
Library of Congress Control Number: 2004094729
ISBN: 1-889910-31-7 (hc)  ISBN: 1-889910-32-5 (pb)

Printing  2  3  4  5  6  7  8  9

Long ago, before there was lightning, stormy nights stayed as black as pitch. Thunder crackled, rain clouds burst. And one fearless boy would run outside to play. Up and down hills, he ran as swiftly as wind.

Once while it stormed, he found villagers gathered before a cave. Strange lights flickered from the cave, and people heard hissing and rattling from within. "That cave has an awful power," warned the boy's father. "Don't go in, or you may never come out."

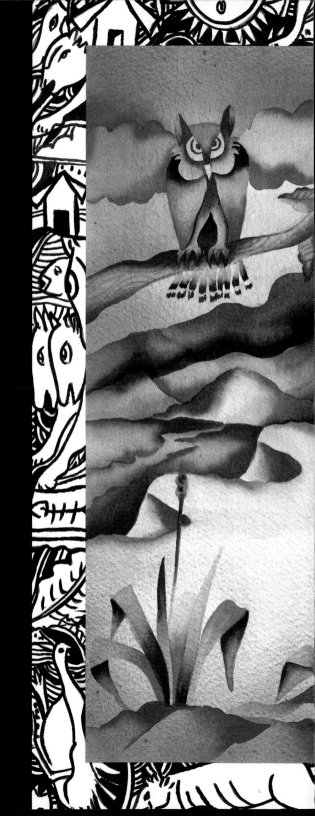

But the warning only made the boy curious, and one day he decided to sneak inside. The air in the cavern smelled damp and stale. Eyes peered out from among the rocks. The boy heard rattling above and below. Suddenly, he saw snakes with human heads, their shiny stripes close enough to touch!

"Who are you?" asked the boy without blinking.

A diamondback waved her body back and forth. She said they were children who had entered the cave, but now they were enchanted and could not leave.

The boy ran home, eager to share his discovery. He was standing in the doorway, catching his breath, when his mother gasped and reached for her grinding stone.

"Go away!" begged his father. "We have nothing for snakes to eat!"

"Do I look like a snake?" the boy asked.

"You certainly have a snake's face!"

The boy reached up and touched his skin. When he told his parents that he had gone into the cave, his mother stroked his head and wept.

"Don't worry," said the boy. "I'll like being a snake."

But the next day when he went to the village market, people rushed away in fear.

The boy's father took him to a *curandero*, an expert in herbs and special cures. The *curandero* burned incense to rid the air of bad spirits. Then he covered the boy's face with wet basil and banana leaves. Still, he could not change him back.

They saw one *curandero* after another. Finally, the boy's father heard talk of a *nahual*, a magic worker who could turn himself into an ocelot or owl. The *nahual* lived on top of a faraway mountain.

"You have been to the forbidden cave," the *nahual* said. He removed a mask from inside his coat. "You must wear this mask for twenty years. And you must dance each year at your village fiesta."

"What will become of my boy?" asked the father.

"The answer," said the *nahual*, "is in the clouds."

The boy wore the mask faithfully as he grew up. As he danced at each summer's fiesta, he prayed for healthy crops so his people would thrive. Children listened eagerly to his stories about the cave. And they cheered "Uncle Snake!" as he ran through the hills whenever rain clouds burst.

After he'd danced for the twentieth year, Uncle Snake returned to the faraway mountain.

"You must go back to the cave," the *nahual* told him. "Stay inside for three days, then go home and take off the mask. You are destined to show the world something new."

The cavern smelled musty, as Uncle Snake had remembered, and again he heard rattling among the rocks.

"We knew you'd come back to *ssee usss*," welcomed the cave snakes.

Uncle Snake told them about the *nahual*. Then he set out offerings to appease the cave's power, which had trapped the cave snakes inside for so long.

Three days passed quickly. "Would you like to go with me?" Uncle Snake asked his friends.

"You go firssst," the cave snakes said timidly, "but don't forget about usss!"

Evening fell as Uncle Snake walked home. Rain clouds gathered as he approached his house. His mother and father came outside to greet him, and children rushed out of their homes to watch.

Thunder cracked as Uncle Snake removed his mask, and at that instant he turned into a snake with a human head.

Thunder clapped overhead again, and this time Uncle Snake leapt into the sky. His zigzagging sheen created a light so brilliant that, for a moment, he turned the night into day.

His family, who had never seen such a spectacle, saw more rays of light shoot out from the cave. The flashes scared children back into their homes just as heavy rain whipped over the land.

In the following years, villagers danced to remember Uncle Snake. And each summer he returned, bringing rain that made crops more abundant than ever.

Today, Uncle Snake still heralds storms. When the sky turns black and the warm winds howl, and rain is about to pour down to the earth in buckets, you can see Uncle Snake too. He streaks across the sky in a flash—and just as quickly, is gone.

# AUTHOR'S NOTE

This story was inspired by an ancient belief in Oaxaca (wa-HAH-ka), Mexico, that a snake in the sky brings about heavy rains. Long ago, people may have perceived such a snake formed by thunderclouds or lightning as storms gathered force. Because snakes shed their skins, they have also symbolized change and rebirth.

In Oaxaca, where electrical storms are common, the ancients regarded lightning as a form of life-giving energy. Lightning generally signals rain—hence fertility and abundance for an agrarian people. Since snakes and lightning both strike quickly, and appear as undulating lines, it is easy to imagine transformation between the two. Some Aztec and Mayan pyramids, found in other regions of Mexico, contain great stone rattlesnakes descending along their ridges to suggest powerful lightning bolts striking the earth. Today in Oaxaca when a lightning storm rages, snakes are said to be "crossing the sky."

Other story elements that figure prominently in pre-Hispanic folklore include:

**CAVE:** Considered an opening to the underworld. Many ancient cultures of Mexico feared the underworld and respected caves as living entities.

**CURANDERO** (coo-rahn-DEH-ro): A folk doctor, or healer, who treats patients with herbs and uses incense to help displace "bad airs." Copal, made from resins of various trees, is especially popular for cleansing the air of evil.

**FIESTA:** A festival that traditionally entails rituals to ensure communal well-being. Sometimes people dance at fiestas to fulfill personal wishes, such as finding a mate or raising healthy children. They dance in later fiestas to show their joy and thanks.

**NAHUAL** (nah-WAL): A shape-changing magic worker both respected and feared, who typically lives in mountains far from other people. The *nahual* is said to divine the future and is considered a medium to the supernatural world.

**OCELOT:** A black-spotted wildcat, smaller than a jaguar or leopard. *Ocelot* comes from Nahuatl, the Aztec language. Other English words borrowed from Nahuatl include *chocolate*, *coyote*, *tomato*, and *shack*.

**OFFERINGS:** Dances or items such as food given to acknowledge favors asked or granted.